PIGS IN HIDING

8 - 99 - 100

Ready or not, here I come.

Nobody here. They must be in the other room.

Nobody here.

Nobody here.

Nobody here
either.

I Know.

They're all upstairs.

OK you guys, I've had enough. You can come out now.
What if they all went home instead of hiding?
I know how to find out if they're still here.

popcorn
donuts
strawberries
peanuts
popcorn
punch
donuts
donuts
punch
punch
strawberries
sandwiches
popcorn

Surprise! I found you.

The End.

I smell popcorn.
I smell peanuts.
donuts

Come out everybody. He's gone.
peanuts
Where is he?
He gave up.
He's gone.
He's gone.
sandwiches
He's gone.